ELISE'S ELATION

Mail Order Bride Christmas Miracles Romance Series
Book 4

KATIE WYATT

ADA OAKLEY

RoyceCardiff
Publishing House
WHOLESOME INSPIRATIONAL ROMANCE

RoyceCardiff
Publishing House
WHOLESOME INSPIRATIONAL ROMANCE

Dear Reader,

It is our utmost pleasure and privilege to bring these wonderful stories to you. I am so very proud of our amazing team of writers and the delight they continually bring us all with their beautiful clean and wholesome tales of, faith, courage, and love.

What is a book's lone purpose if not to be read and enjoyed? Therefore, you, dear reader, are the key to fulfilling that purpose and unlocking the treasures that lie within the pages of this book.

NEWSLETTER SIGN UP GET FREE BOOKS!

http://katieWyattBooks.com/readersgroup

CONTENTS

A PERSONAL WORD FROM KATIE

I LOVE WRITING ABOUT THE OLD WEST AND THE trials, tribulations, and triumphs of the early pioneer women.

With strong fortitude and willpower, they took a big leap of faith believing in the promised land of the West. It was always not a bed of roses, however many found true love.

Most of the stories are based on some historical fact or personal conversations I've had with folks who knew something of that time. For example a relative of the Wyatt Earp's. I have spent much time out in the West camping hiking and carousing. I have spent countless hours gazing up at night thinking of how it must been back then.

Thank you for being a loyal reader.

Katie

Mail Order Bride Christmas Miracles Romance

Book 1 Leigh's Love
Book 2 Melanie's Miracle
Book 3 Felicity's Folly
Book 4 Elise's Elation

CHAPTER 1

At the mention of heaven, Elise Schmidt's voice broke a little.

Dressed in a cotton dress hastily dyed black only the day before, Elise stood quietly at the front of First Lutheran Trinity Church, a small book of prayers clutched in her gloved hands. The interior of the church was ice cold, as were her insides. The presiding parson, Pastor Doederlein, raised his hands over an imaginary congregation; aside from Mrs. Brown, owner of the tiny boarding house where her aunt had spent her last days before going to hospital, and Elise herself, the church was empty. Elise felt a trail of warm wetness make its way down one cheek, and she bit her lip hard to keep a sob from escaping.

I'm so sorry I was not with you, Tante.

The tears were falling faster now, slipping down over the bridge of her nose, into the high collar of her dress. Elise had not cried up until this point—not when she'd visited the hospital to speak to the doctors, not when she had been told her aunt's body, unclaimed for weeks, had been already buried by the city, and not even when she discovered that Tante's small house had been auctioned off by her lawyers to pay off her medical bills.

Elise had arrived in Chicago only three weeks ago, grimy and exhausted from a journey from Germany that had taken her from ship to rail, from New York City to Illinois, nothing but a scrap of paper in her reticule with her aunt's address on it. She found the woman dead from the breathing sickness that had plagued her since her days as a young woman in Luxembourg. Elise had not had time to mourn; she had arrangements to make, letters to write, a memorial service to arrange. Now, under the kindly eye of

Reverend Doederlein, she could finally give her aunt a proper farewell.

"Amen," the reverend said quietly, and Elise realized with a jolt that he was at the end of the service. She took a deep, shaky breath, closed her eyes briefly, and opened them to see Mrs. Brown looking at her, a kind expression in her soft gray eyes.

"Oh, my child," she said, and reached out and touched Elise's cheek. "Let's go home."

❧

CHICAGO, OF COURSE, WAS NOT HOME FOR ELISE. IT was a strange city, with its teeming streets and strange smells and chimneys that painted the sky with smudges of heavy black smoke. Mrs. Brown's boarding house, though clean and respectable, was in a grimy corner of the industrial area that secretly horrified Elise. It was a terrible place for a woman with a lung condition to have spent the last few months of her life—and with no one to care for her, either! The thought that her aunt had suffered and died alone, with no family whatsoever to comfort or to care for her, hurt Elise deeply.

"Come to the kitchen and have something to eat," Mrs. Brown invited. "You're looking mighty peaky, child. You didn't have a bite to eat for breakfast."

Elise managed a watery smile. "*Danke schoen*," she said softly.

"You sound just like Miss Schmidt, bless her," the good woman said warmly, and hustled Elise into her big homey kitchen, from which savory smells emitted. She spooned a generous serving of that afternoon's beef stew into a large bowl, poured a glass of buttermilk, and took out biscuits that had been keeping warm at the back of her cookstove, along with a crock of honey that Elise knew she normally reserved for Sundays. She gave Mrs. Brown a grateful look and began to eat, methodically. She wasn't hungry, not in the least, but she could not waste the woman's food or spurn her kindness.

Mrs. Brown watched her like a hawk for several moments. When the spoon had passed from bowl to mouth enough times to apparently pass muster, she relaxed.

"What will you do now, Elise?" she inquired.

Elise placed her spoon on the table and reached up to touch her temples with her fingertips, rubbing as if she could persuade her brain to come up with the necessary answers through touch. "I don't know," she admitted. "*Mein vater* intended for me to live with Tante. I don't know what..." she trailed off helplessly. "How long had she been this way? I was always told she was a successful dressmaker here in the city."

"Milliner," Mrs. Brown corrected, "and she was quite successful, until she became ill. I purchased one or two of her best for my Sunday wear. Such lovely bonnets," she added to herself, shaking her head gravely.

Elise bit her lip. "She said nothing to Papa."

"She was his older sister," Mrs. Brown said gently. "She didn't want to be a burden. Pick up your spoon, child. Eat up."

Elise followed her instructions, somewhat woodenly. "I don't know what I am to do," she said, half to herself, half to Mrs. Brown.

"Can you not write your father and have him pay for your passage home?"

Elise shook her head. She did not have the energy to explain her situation to Mrs. Brown—she did not expect this kindly American to understand the sort of danger she was in, as the daughter of a Lutheran minister in Germany. She barely understood it herself; all she knew was that her father had suggested, his face dark, that she might want to spend some time in America with his sister, until it was safe to bring her back. Elise had not asked for details; he had not offered them. She had written him as soon as she arrived but had heard nothing back yet.

"My father is unable to do so," was all she said.

Mrs. Brown merely nodded, tapping her fingertips on the tabletop. Her face was thoughtful. Her fingers went to the money bag at her waist.

"Your aunt," she said slowly, "paid for her room until the end of the month. You are welcome to stay until then."

Gratefully, Elise thanked her, then realized the woman's unsaid meaning. She would likely need to pay after that, or she would have to leave. She felt her stomach knot.

"Mrs. Brown," she said, and her voice was quiet. "I realize this may be a terrible time to ask, but is there any possibility..."

The older woman was already shaking her head. "I ain't got anything at the moment," she said frankly.

"I'd like to help you. I truly would. Your aunt was a good woman, but it's all I can do to make ends meet myself. But I do have an odd sort of idea, if you're keen to listen…"

❧

MAIL ORDER MARRIAGE WAS NOT A CONCEPT THAT was foreign to Elise; she knew many girls back home that had struck out for new lands in exchange for the financial security of marriage. The concept, however, had never been one she thought she might apply to herself. She was Elise Schmidt, daughter of a respected minister in their tiny community just outside Berlin; when she chose to marry, likely when she was much older than the nineteen years of age she'd recently celebrated, it would be a man she respected and loved, a man of her own choosing. Well. That was what she'd always thought, anyway.

As it stands, you are choosing him, in a way…

Elise fought back a near-hysterical urge to laugh, sitting cross-legged on the floor of her aunt's tiny room in Mrs. Brown's building. Her skirts were tucked beneath her, and she was scanning the advertisement section of several papers, some purchased with Elise's dwindling savings that morning, others obtained from Mrs. Brown, who had clipped them, helpfully.

"You might as well just get married," Mrs. Brown had said the day before, opening that morning's *Daily Standard* as an example. "My Elizabeth married and moved to California last spring, she did. Married a fine farmer, a man with orange trees on his property. Lizzie writes me once a week." She paused, clearly remembering her daughter with fondness. "They have a baby already. Big, fat boy. A young lady like you could do much worse."

"Marry a stranger?" Elise was shocked.

Mrs. Brown huffed. "Men and women are all strangers to each other until they live together, young miss. Take my word for it."

Elise had lain awake much of that night, thinking hard. Then she'd gotten up at four and prayed fervently.

Lord, if this is indeed what I am to do, guide my steps, please.

Now, she peered down at the smudged print of the ads in front of her. Thanks to her father's insistence on an excellent education for his daughter, Elise read English well, but slowly, and most of the ads were fairly straightforward. *Man seeks woman.* Some specified hair color or eye color. Others were more particular about age. Some were old, some young. Some used flowery language; others attempted humor. It was fascinating, but utterly confusing, until one ad jumped out at her with a jolt of familiarity that stole her breath.

Fraulein wanted as wife to banker in the state of Montana. Must speak both English and German equally well.

The lines were repeated in German. Elise let the paper slide to her lap, took a deep, shaky breath, and leaned back.

Is this a sign, Lord?

CHAPTER 2

His name was Adam Hornick.

On her weeks-long trip out west, Elise had many hours to test the name on her tongue, to practice writing it in the margins of the exercise books she used as journals.

Adam Hornick.

The very afternoon she'd seen the ad, she scrawled a short, badly spelled, ink-smudged letter, a dreadfully short letter in an incongruous mix of English and German, giving her name, her age, and exactly why she was looking for a husband. If this was indeed to be her fate, she intended to start by being completely honest. She waited in breathless anticipation for two weeks, and received a letter, as informal and as businesslike as the first had been.

"Dear Miss Schmidt," the letter said,

Thank you for your prompt and frank response; I appreciate those qualities in a woman. I will be frank with you. I advertised for a German-speaking wife to care for my ailing mother, who lives with me here. She has only lived in German-speaking communities until now, and feels ill at ease with English-speaking caretakers whom she cannot express herself to readily. I am not always available to aid her in translation, and at times she wishes to discuss delicate matters about her health with her caretakers, which she finds it distressing for me to hear.

I am a man of good standing in my community, and will treat you with the utmost regard and respect. If you choose to take this position, I will ensure your needs are met, and you will be comfortable and well-treated.

I have enclosed a photograph of myself, as well as letters of reference from my pastor and the town sheriff. You are free to correspond with both independently, of course. However, since your letter seemed to indicate that your position is somewhat precarious, I have taken the liberty of including provisions for your trip here to Montana in this letter. Should you choose to use them, you may write me and set out immediately. Should you wish to correspond more, that is also agreeable.

I eagerly await your response.

I am your servant,

Adam Frederick Hornick.

His photo had been sharp and clear; a man who looked to be in his early thirties stared at the camera almost defiantly, holding his hat in his hand. Even from the photograph, his eyes burned a clear light color; blue, Elise supposed, like hers. His hair was the blinding shade of white often only seen in little children, parted, and smoothed flat on his head.

He was handsome, she thought with a little flip of the heart. In a very stern head-masterish sort of way, but still handsome. It was so hard to tell anything about a person from a mere image on a glossy bit of paper. If she allowed herself to think about it, to really think about it, she would be terrified. This was a man she would presumably share her life with.

Many times while on her journey, Elise prayed for strength, for courage that would take her through the days ahead. However, as she peered through the sooty windows of train and stagecoach cars, watching as the country flashed green and brown and blue on either side, she felt a rush of excitement that grew with every passing day until, at long last, the end of her travels came into view over a wide, flat landscape.

Blue Ridge, Montana, the conductor on the train during the last leg of her journey told her, was a tiny town. "It's really little more than a feeding post for the farms around it, ma'am," he said. "I've only been there once, and wasn't much there."

"Is it pleasant?"

"Pleasant enough, and growing. I can tell you—it's one of the prettiest parcels of land around these parts. You won't be doing much wandering about now that it's cold, but in the summer..." the man let out a low, appreciative whistle. "The locals call it Violet Vale. It's really something to behold, miss."

"Thank you," Elise replied, her heart beating fast. In her hand she turned Adam's photograph over and over; the conductor caught sight of it and smiled kindly.

"Meeting a relative?"

"My fiancé," said Elise, blushing profusely.

"Congrats." The man tipped his hat before heading off to attend to the other people on the train.

The train arrived in good time, the locomotive blowing steam into the frigid air. Elise was glad for her warm coat, mittens, hat, and scarf—all lined with fur, brought in her trunk from Germany. The ground at the depot was frozen hard and barren, decorated with patches of snow. Elise patted her cheeks, thankful for the weather; they should flush becomingly, at least.

"Good luck, miss," the conductor said as he helped her down from the train. A boy in a red cap ran forward to unload the battered trunk that held all her worldly possessions. When both she and her things were settled safely on the platform, Elise fumbled inside her coat for the soft leather pouch that served as a reticule while she traveled.

"Please wait," she told the boy, straining for the coins that she knew were tucked inside the bag. "I'd like to give you something for your kind assistance—"

"I'll take care of that," a voice said, very close to her ear. It was a rich baritone, tinged with the vowels Elise remembered from home; they were softened, blunted around the edges, but they were there. She looked up in confusion to see a man in a black coat, brown wool mittens, and scarf, looking down at her. Elise's breath caught in her lungs as his mouth tipped up at the edges, just a little.

Had he observed her reaction? She didn't think so; it was too cold.

His eyes were blue, as she had guessed—bright and clear as the sea. When he lifted his hat after giving the boy a few coins, that white-blond hair shone even in the weak, watery light of winter.

"Adam Hornick," he said simply. "Hello, Miss Schmidt."

Elise nodded in acknowledgment; she felt a sudden urge to curtsy, which would have been ridiculous, but there was something so imposing about Adam, it practically demanded it. "Herr Hornick," she said softly.

He shook his head, looking not quite pleased about something, but she, of course, did not know him well enough to guess what it might be. "Adam is fine. Do come with me," and they walked together to the wagon that sat a few meters away, a large black horse waiting patiently, its breath steaming up the air. "Are you warm enough?"

Elise nodded dumbly, then forced herself to speak. In English. The words came out rather clumsily as she did not have time to ponder them before speaking, but with Adam speaking to her in English, it felt awkward attempting anything else.

"I am quite warm, thank you."

He nodded, then gripped her hand to help her into the wagon. At the same time, another man appeared on the other side of the wagon and heaved Elise's trunk in, then vanished back into the crowd. Adam's hands were strong and capable, and yet he handled her as carefully as if she were made of glass.

"Mind your feet," he said mildly, and knelt to lift them up one by one. Elise felt a shock of warmth through the bottom of her boots, and peered down.

"Bricks," he said. "We heat them in the stove and wrap them in feedbags, to use to keep warm on long drives. Old farmer's trick."

"Danke," she said.

There it was, that look again—just a flicker of displeasure, but it was unmistakable this time. "Your English is very good," Adam said, shaking the reins, seeming to imply something, though what, Elise couldn't fathom.

The horse snorted, then plodded forward.

"I studied in a mission school," she replied. "It was run by an Englishman who came to Berlin."

Adam looked at her then, fixing those inscrutable blue eyes on her face. There was a mixture of curiosity, sympathy, and something else that lit a warm fire in her chest, spreading out to her fingers.

Whatever he may be, he is kind, at least, she thought. She could see it in his expression even before he said his next words.

"I am truly sorry for your difficulties, and I pray every day for the health and safety of your father and the rest of your family," he said.

Simple words, but they brought tears to Elise's eyes. She had not cried since the memorial service; she had been afraid that if she started, she'd never stop. Adam reached out hesitantly, then patted her hand where it sat between them, atop the lap blanket. Between all the layers of wool and fur, it was impossible to even speculate about what his skin felt like, but the gesture was comforting. She took a deep breath and got ahold of herself.

"Thank you, Adam," she said softly.

He smiled then, just a little. It was nowhere as bright as she would have hoped, but it was enough for Elise, for the moment.

CHAPTER 3

BLUE RIDGE WAS TINY, ALMOST SHOCKINGLY SO.
"In summer," Adam told her, "boys make wagers on who can race from one end to the other the fastest. It doesn't take long." His house was one of the finest in the small town. It was a red-brick structure adjacent to the bank, with hunter-green shutters and a neatly swept front stoop.

"Most of the folks in Blue Ridge are homesteaders. Farmers. Cattle ranchers. We've got a couple of shops, a dressmaker, a butcher, a bank, and of course, a church," Adam said as he helped her down from the wagon. "We'll head over there later, meet the reverend." He cleared his throat. "I took the liberty of sending for the Lutheran order of service for our wedding. I know it holds some significance for you."

For the second time that afternoon, Elise felt tears brim in her eyes. "Thank you."

Adam opened his mouth to reply, but the door flew open, and a small, plump woman stood just inside, beaming at both of them.

"*Frauelein, wie gehts?*" she cried.

"Mama, close the door!" Adam switched to German, and Elise followed his lead, saying, "*Guten abend, Mama,*" and curtsying, as she had been brought up to do.

Mama was not so very old, but despite her plumpness she was pale and moved slowly; just from those few minutes of excitement, beads of sweat stood out on her forehead. Elise immediately worried for the woman and wondered if it was her heart.

"Mama, please sit down," she said in German, and the woman's round face creased into a smile.

"*Ach,* I thought I would never hear my language from a child's lips again," she said, and patted Elise's cheek. "Come, come. You must be tired and hungry. Adam insists you go to church tonight, but there is no reason why you cannot have something to eat before going." She hustled the pair to a small but elegantly furnished dining room off the front hall. The table was spread simply. *"Kaffee und kuchen,"* the older woman said grandly, and indeed, it was! The table was spread with as many cakes as would fit, piled high with whipped cream and sprinkled with cinnamon, nutmeg, chocolate shavings.

"This looks just like home!" Elise exclaimed, eyes widening with delight. "Thank you so much."

"It is my pleasure."

"You must let me cook for you tomorrow, Mama. Perhaps sauerbraten with noodles, if your health allows."

Mama beamed and patted Elise's arm. "I'll see to it that it does!"

"I am hoping my cooking will be able to tempt your appetite," Elise returned. "I can make nearly any German dish."

"You will have to learn some American ones, too," Adam said in that quiet way of his. He sliced cake, added a generous spoonful of whipped cream, and passed the plate to Elise. Once again, Elise caught a hint of a confusing undertone that she didn't understand.

Mama snorted but refrained from commenting. The three ate, talked, and laughed for an hour, and then Adam stood.

"We must not keep the parson waiting."

It was a quick walk from the Hornick residence over to the church, a tiny clapboard structure with a steepled roof. It was the first building in Blue Ridge, Adam told Elise, and one that meant much to the residents of the tiny town. "The schoolhouse is built in much the same style." He'd reverted to the formal, stilted English he'd used when he collected her at the station. Elise's heart was already pounding at the thought of the wedding, and it beat that much faster as her worry grew steadily that something wasn't quite right that she couldn't put her finger on.

As they walked, Adam offered her his arm in an old-fashioned gesture that suited him; she could feel the strength of his muscles even through the thick wool, and again felt that overwhelming peace, that inner assurance that, yes, in spite of the subtle hint of a problem, she was safe here, with this man God had guided her to.

When they reached the door of the church, Adam hesitated, then reached into his pocket and drew out a small pouch of deer hide. It was simply but beautifully tooled, with what Elise guessed were hand-stitched seams.

"A box would have been more elegant, but this was all I could find," he apologized. "Open it."

Elise pulled a mitten off and did so. Inside, wrapped in a scrap of sky-blue silk, was a pearl and opal ring.

"It was Mama's," he said quietly over her exclamations. "I would like very much for you to be happy, Elise. I know this marriage was born out of necessity, but I intend to forge forward as if it wasn't, if you will allow me."

Elise bit her lip. Her heart was too full to speak, so she laid her hand in Adam's, handing him the ring back hopefully.

His mouth twitched. "I believe we might want to wait for the parson," he said, but he slid the cool circle of metal up her ring finger. "It fits perfectly."

"Ja," Elise said softly; she had no other words, not at the moment. She could feel her eyes welling with tears. Adam saw them and peered into her face.

"Dear Elise," he said, and his voice was heavy with compassion. "I'm so sorry for what brought you here."

Elise nodded rapidly. Tears were escaping her eyes now at the memory of the persecution she and her family had suffered, running warm and wet down her cheeks, one by one. "I am sorry," she choked out. "I'm not sure why I'm so emotional. I—"

Adam shook his head and dragged his hat off his head, one big hand resting lightly on her shoulder and sending warmth through her from head to toe. "Elise," he said. His voice was tense with so much feeling that it further warmed her from the inside, completely obliterating the cold around them. "I am not perfect. I will say that now. However, I want you to consider me family, just as much as those you left behind."

"Thank you, Adam," Elise said, and she impulsively stood on her toes and kissed him.

They were on the porch of a church, and the wind was making them both shiver, and her nose was running terribly, and this was not at all the thing for a lady to do, but—well. She wanted to. She did not want to start this marriage by hiding anything from her husband, least of all the fact that she had been touched by his kindness and suddenly wanted to kiss him very badly.

After stiffening in surprise, Adam kissed her back. It was warm and slow and unbelievably tender, and when he pulled back seconds later, Elise had a lump in her throat for reasons other than missing her family.

He was looking down at her, an odd look on his face. He pulled out a pocket handkerchief and handed it to her.

"Dry your face," he suggested. "We should get inside."

"All right," she said shakily, and mopped at her face with the square of white cloth. Adam reached down, took her hand in his large warm grip, and together they stepped forward into their new life.

CHAPTER 4

"I CAN SEE," JUNE BAKER SAID CHEERFULLY, "WHY Adam took you to wife. What a lovely figure you have, dear!"

It was a bright Monday morning, only a week after Elise and Adam's wedding, and she was finally beginning to feel settled in the tiny town. Mama had spent three nights with the parson and his wife in a bid to give the newlyweds some privacy. Adam promised her a proper honeymoon as soon as spring came, but Elise was content. She spent those first three days exploring the small, charming house, with its old elegant furniture and quiet, refined touches that reflected its owner.

But now she'd left the relative sanctuary of her husband's home to explore what it meant to be a banker's wife. Adam had ordered her a new wardrobe, and Elise now stood shivering in her chemise and petticoats in the main room of the town's one dressmaker. June Baker was married to the town schoolteacher, and was a plump, pretty woman of thirty years who'd come out with her husband from Boston.

"I thought it a grand adventure," she said gaily. "And here I am. I am so glad you've joined us, dear. There's very little here by way of female company in this town. We all must help each other."

Adam, Elise had learned, was not only a banker of good standing in town—he was running for mayor. He'd told her this over a simple supper of meat, bread, cheese, and *kuchen* the day before. When she shared this with June now, the little woman nodded emphatically.

"He wished me to outfit you in a manner suited to a mayor's wife," she admitted, attacking Elise's slim waist and hips with her measuring tape. "Not that there's much to show off for in this place! His only opponent is the sitting mayor, Jeb Winters. He's fifty if he is a day and complains about how winter makes his bones ache at every town meeting. A good man, but I think he'd hand your husband his seat and leave town tomorrow if he could."

"Adam says the town will grow quickly and needs strong leadership."

"He isn't wrong about that. Homesteaders are pouring in by the wagonful every week, and folks are consistently coming off the train and disappearing into the grasslands. In another ten years, Blue Ridge will be almost unrecognizable." June motioned for Elise to button herself back into the dark-brown wool dress with red piping she'd arrived in. "Adam said you were fair, so I chose gray, slate, and several shades of blue." As she spoke, June draped material of incredibly rich hues and softness over her worktable. "Perhaps a dusty rose as well, to bring out the color in your cheeks."

"He ordered this ahead of time?" Elise asked in surprise.

"Oh yes, weeks ahead."

Interesting. So Adam had put things in place, even before she'd come, or had said yes. That sounded very much like Adam. Elise smiled. Her fingers lingered on a bolt of lace; the soft, delicate fabric would make a lovely fichu and mob cab. Her mother-in-law was one of the best things about Blue Ridge so far; the older woman was kind, thoughtful, and determined to stuff her new daughter-in-law with the richest meals imaginable.

"Would you like a lace edge on one of the dresses, Mrs. Hornick?"

Elise was a bit startled; she was still unused to being called Mrs. anything. "No, actually, my mother-in-law has a birthday soon," she said. "I was thinking this lace might do for a lovely set of caps for her. Normally I would knit it, but I haven't time."

"You have a good eye," June praised. "Brussels lace is some of the finest. Shall I cut a piece for you?"

Elise hesitated. She and Adam still had not had a discussion over finances; she hated to put anything on his account without his permission. "I will wait, but thank you," she said, and placed a hand on the woman's arm. "I promise to come back here when I do buy."

"You'll have to; this is the only place in town!" the woman laughed. She paused, then took down her shears, measured two yards of the expensive lace, and cut. "Wedding present," she said with a wink. "The remainder would be fine edging on a nightgown."

Elise smiled and thanked God again for the kindness of people who, just days ago, had been strangers.

WHEN ELISE FINISHED WITH JUNE, SHE RAN lightly across the street to the bank, the package of lace tightly tucked under one arm. She'd glanced at the clock before leaving; it was a quarter to five, and she knew that Adam would be closing up shortly. Perhaps she would surprise him at work and walk him home. She pushed open the large gilt door with only a little hesitance, and entered.

She saw Adam almost immediately—his was the lightest head in the room, and he was bent over a ledger in a pool of four desks, all occupied by men as somberly dressed as he was. Elise hesitated, not wanting to interrupt; they all looked so busy. However, as if her thoughts called out to him, her husband raised his head. He looked surprised, but to Elise's relief, he smiled.

"Come here," he mouthed, lifting a hand. Elise picked up her skirts and navigated the room as silently as possible.

"*Wie ghets*...darling?" she said when she arrived at his side, trying out the new endearment on her tongue. Adam's brows rose in alarm.

"Not here, Elise," he hissed under his breath, looking around at his companions, who were all diligently scratching away at papers in front of them. At the hurt, confused look that Elise was not quite able to hide, he sighed. "Please wait. I will be ready to walk you home in ten minutes."

Blinking back tears, she nodded and fled for the door. She considered running home and going straight to bed, but she did not; instead she stood shivering in the foyer. A sensible person would have remained within reach of the bank's coal heater or sat on one of the chairs in the receiving area, but she was too troubled. She remembered her father's words, both at home and behind the pulpit:

You must find the courage to face your fears, for they will still exist if you don't.

She was not afraid of Adam; his consideration and his kindness made that impossible. However, she was terrified of the fact that already, her heart was tied to him. And yet she knew that, underneath it all, that untapped question she'd had since their wedding day remained unanswered. They'd been so happy—she'd been afraid to broach the subject, and even told herself she'd imagined it. Well, clearly she hadn't.

When Adam exited his office, coat on and hat in hand, Elise had managed to pull herself together once more. She would not, she told herself, feel bad about this.

I have done nothing wrong.

"You should have waited inside," Adam said.

"I enjoy the fresh air."

"It's very cold."

The air was not the only cold thing she had experienced that evening, she could have said, but she decided not to. Instead she pulled her muffler over her mouth and nose, and the two exited into the frigid wind.

They walked side by side, silently, until Adam spoke. "I'm sorry about that, Elise." He did not have to explain what he was referring to; they both knew.

"Why?" Elise asked after a moment, finally asking the question in her heart.

He sighed. "We're in America now, Elise, and I am doing my best to prove to my customers and future constituents that I am a thoroughly American candidate, and have integrated myself fully into society. That can't happen if you're speaking to me in

German in public. That's the only thing they will remember, and—"

Bewildered, Elise stopped and looked up at him. She honestly hadn't had any idea why he was upset, and this? This was the last thing she expected. "That was about speaking German?"

Adam looked down at her, confused. "What else would it be about, Elise?"

"I thought that perhaps you didn't want—" she hesitated. "I surprised you, and—"

He stared at her for another full moment; then, realization dawned. "No—no," he insisted, looking horrified. "I—no, Elise. I was absolutely thrilled to see you. Elise." He stopped short so that the two of them stood in the middle of the street, and bent so that he could look her right in the eye. "You are my wife," he said forcefully. "You have every right to be wherever I am."

At his look, Elise felt a rush of relief so intense she actually felt a little dizzy. "I—" she began.

Adam took one quick glance around to see who was in the street, then bent to kiss her swiftly on the lips. "Let's have no more of that!" he said.

Elise smiled, although weakly. Whatever relief she felt was muted by the fact that, once again, they hadn't discussed the actual problem. And now that she knew it was her language, she was even more confused. However, Adam had quickened his steps, undoubtedly eager to get home to a warm stove and a hot dinner, and Elise chose not to belabor the point for now.

I will talk to him later, she promised herself.

CHAPTER 5

WHEN ELISE HAD BEEN MARRIED A MONTH, JUNE Baker announced that she was throwing a dinner for her. "Just an informal welcome to Blue Ridge, darling, nothing else." This "informal welcome" turned out to be an excuse for the good woman to showcase the fine china and gleaming white tablecloths she'd brought from back east, as well as to gather the town's most influential couples in one room to dine. Along with the Hornicks and the Bakers, there were the Cooks—the husband-and-wife team that ran the town's main dry goods store—along with Parson Samuels and his sweet wife Hannah.

June's dining room was large and airy, and warmed nicely by a coal grate tucked discreetly behind an iron panel. At the dinner, Elise debuted the dusty-rose cashmere dress June had made for her, with pinned pale silk roses in her hair. She was gratified to hear her husband's intake of breath when he saw her.

"You look lovely," Adam said gravely, and held her cloak with its lining of watered-blue silk for her, then handed Elise her hat and her muff. It felt odd to wear such fine clothing; Elise's father had been an advocate of sober dress. Still, she looked at herself in the mirror with more than a little satisfaction.

"It's all your doing," she said cheerfully, holding out her skirts and waltzing about. He did laugh then, and Elise prayed inwardly that his lighthearted mood would continue throughout their evening. They hadn't yet talked. She just didn't have the courage to broach the confusing subject.

Elise was given the seat of honor, closest to the heat, and the evening was lighthearted and fun, beginning with parlor games and a brief lecture by Mr. Baker, followed by a four-course dinner, served up in style on June's English china. Afterward, Hannah Samuels played the organ.

"You all must sing," invited June. "Even you, Mr. Hornick," she told Adam teasingly.

He laughed. The food and good company seemed to have lightened him up quite a bit. "I am many things, but not a talented musician, I am afraid."

"Do you play, Mrs. Hornick?"

"Only a little," Elise replied with a smile. "My father is a member of the clergy, so we always had music in church. I sing much better than I play, although I fear my repertoire is limited to hymns."

"This was in—Berlin, was it?" Mr. Cook said jovially. His round face was flushed with the warmth and good food. "Wonderful food, your people have."

Elise could feel her husband stiffen at her side. *What now? He dislikes the language AND the food?* "German food is delicious, though it does tend to make one stout."

"No worries, I'm there already." He patted his girth again, and the crowd laughed.

"You must treat us," said June, "to one of those songs, after we eat."

"Oh," Elise said uncertainly. "I do not want to take Hannah's turn—"

"Heavens!" said Hannah cheerfully. "I would be more than glad to accompany you, dear."

The company pressed her, and Elise looked a little helplessly at Adam. He smiled.

"As I have never heard her sing, this will be an uncommon treat for me as well," he said after a short pause. Everyone chuckled.

"We will look forward to it, then," June said with a grin, and lifted her glass.

❧

AFTER DINNER, THE SMALL GROUP RETIRED TO THE parlor, and Hannah took her seat at the organ's tall stool. There was no sheet music, but Hannah needed none; years of accompanying singers in church and at town social events had given her an ear to rival any concert pianist. She nodded in Elise's direction, and the latter cleared her throat, then began to sing of God, of heaven, of His eyes looking down.

"Ach Gott, vom Himmel sieh darein..."

Elise's voice was as sweet, as plaintive as a harp. As she sang, she thought of the simple building she'd gone to every Sunday, of her father's rolling baritone, of the love and tenderness with which he treated his parishioners. By the end of the song, her throat was so constricted that she nearly could not finish, in part by homesickness and also with the dread that Adam might disapprove of the language she'd used. But she knew no songs in English. What else could she do?

She discreetly whisked away a tear, hurrying to sit at her husband's side. He gave her a look that was inscrutable but thankfully lacking in anger. Then Adam took her hand, drawing it up and kissing her knuckles lightly.

"I should thank you all," he said to the assembled company, "for encouraging her to sing. You sounded absolutely beautiful, my darling."

Elise almost cried again with relief as the small party clapped vigorously. Later on, as coffee and cake were handed around, June hurried over and spoke for Elise's ears only.

"I'm sorry if I made you sad," she whispered, looking around to make sure no one overheard them. "I should have known, as you've just arrived. Oh—can you forgive me, Elise?"

Elise gripped her hand tight. "Don't even give it a second thought," she said, and even managed a watery smile. "I just miss home very much."

"Understandably!" June clucked, then kissed her friend's cheek and pressed a second plate of cake on her. "You must," she said, straightening up and addressing Adam, "take very good care of her. Homesickness is so very painful."

"I will do my best to ensure she becomes a good and happy American," he said after a long moment.

AS THEY STROLLED HOME UNDER THE COVER OF ICY darkness, Elise found herself humming the hymn again, under her breath. It had been her father's favorite, and now she closed her eyes. She knew he could not hear her thoughts, and she would write to him soon, but—

I miss you so much, Papa, she thought. *Adam is a good man, and I think I will be happy here. But I miss you.*

Adam was silent during most of their walk. He smiled a little when she exclaimed over the fat white flakes of snow that began drifting down, and he responded to all her questions and statements with his usual gentle consideration. However, when they reached the steps of their house, he turned towards her, his face suddenly tight and angry, and Elise's heart sank.

"Why," he said, "do you insist on opposing my wishes?"

"Adam," she began, but he barged on.

"The talk about Berlin. And the singing. And the—"

"June asked, Adam," Elise pointed out.

"You should have politely put her off! If we are to be thought of as an *American* couple, we must—"

"Deny who I really am?" Elise said, tears rising thick in her throat. "Pretend that Elise Schmidt has no ties whatsoever with Germany? Perhaps June would have been a better wife for you, then."

The words cut through the frigid air, harsh and angry, and the two stared at each other for a moment before Adam reached over and opened the door.

"After you," he said icily.

Elise ducked beneath his arm and ran into the house. She avoided Mama, who was seated in her easy chair by the fire, and instead went straight to their bedroom, lying down on the clean white counterpane. Her head was spinning, and she closed her eyes.

She had no idea how much time had passed—minutes or hours—before Adam came in. She did not open her eyes, but she could spell something spicy.

"Sassafras tea," her husband said quietly, and placed something beside her on the table next to the bed. "Mama made a batch; she thought it would be good, on a night like this."

Elise did not respond.

Adam sighed, and Elise felt the bed dip as he sat beside her.

"Elise."

She said nothing.

"I am sorry, Elise. It was badly said."

"And yet, you meant it."

"Yes, I did. Every word."

At that, Elise sat bolt upright in bed, eyes blazing. "Are you ashamed of me then, husband?"

She was gratified to see horror cross his face—only for a split second, but it was there. "No!" he said forcefully, closing the distance to grasp her hands in his. "I am not. I just—Elise, you are new to this country and do not know what...Being different is not always ideal, especially in a town like Blue Ridge, and I want neither I nor my wife to be seen as mere curiosities."

Each word was like a stone, dropping down with a dull thud Elise felt in the innermost recesses of her heart. "A curiosity?" she said softly. "Is that what you think of me, Adam?"

He exhaled, a short, frustrated sound. "Of course not."

Elise felt a little like she was moving outside her own body as she sat up slowly. Adam was seated next to her in his nightshirt, his hair rumpled on his head, his blue eyes pleading but immovable. Something in her constricted despite herself; he was so handsome, and the memories of his tenderness to her these past weeks made it all the more difficult to remain angry. Were he a cruel man, this would be easier to accept. But at the same time, his pigheadedness was such a contrast to his usual kind nature that it was doubly bewildering.

Wordlessly, she shifted forward, and Adam took her into his arms with a sigh. She placed her head on his chest. She could feel the warmth of his skin through the thin material, hearing the low, steady beat of his heart.

"I am sorry," he said after a moment.

She said nothing. His apology did not mean he thought his words had been wrong, and they both knew it.

CHAPTER 6

THE FIRST FEW WEEKS TURNED INTO THE FIRST month, and the second, and Elise found herself facing her first Christmas in America with what seemed like very little warning. After their clash the evening of June's dinner party, Elise had done her best to please her husband. She dressed impeccably, joined the Ladies' Aid Society, hosted teas and suppers and entertainments, all carefully as American as possible.

She only spoke German to Mama, whom she cared for tenderly, and to her father, who she wrote to once a week. Adam was kind to her as always—even attentive, but the harsh disagreement still hung between them, threatening to break open the little cocoon of serenity they had managed to wrap themselves in, for the moment. The fact that Elise's heart jumped a little every time she saw him made it even worse;

Adam only grew handsomer to her as the weeks progressed, and there were other things to admire about him—his gentle strength, his plans for Blue Ridge.

"I want," he said fiercely one night as they huddled together in bed, clinging to each other against a howling wind, "to make Blue Ridge a prosperous, beautiful town, a refuge for anyone who wishes to come here." The irony of the statement made Elise bite her tongue, but bite her tongue she did.

She remembered the admonition from her father's big Bible almost as well as she remembered him, and she was determined that this belief of Adam's would not cause dissension in their home. Her job was to support him as his wife, regardless of his strange ideas. But a small voice inside her did wonder if it wasn't also a husband's job to do the same in turn.

After much prayer, seeking her father's advice seemed a natural next step, and Elise, unable to hold back anymore, poured her heart out to her father in a long, tense letter, stained with blots where tears had fallen. She received an answer back, and read it with an aching heart.

My dear daughter,

It grieves me to know that you are so unhappy, although I do believe Adam Hornick is a good man. Behavior that seems irrational to us is often as a result of hidden hurts, and as he otherwise is good to you, I think there may be something there that he cannot, or will not, share with you.

My dear, I would advise you to pray for your husband and show him respect and love without losing sight of yourself. Talk to your mother-in-law; she seems an advocate and will know her son better than you can at this point. I pray for you every day, and regret that you are presently unhappy. Know that God does have a plan for you and will see it through in His own time.

I am forever,

your loving Papa.

Elise folded the letter with tearful eyes, then tucked it away where she could reread it, to comfort herself when she missed him. Mama, though kind and loving, was as reticent as her son; when asked, she shook her white head.

"It is not my story to tell," was all she would say, and so, Elise was left to wonder.

WITH DECEMBER CAME ADVENT, AND WITH Advent came a considerable lifting of Elise's spirits, despite herself. Adam's dislike of his German heritage did not extend to the birth of the *Christkind*, and Elise found herself humming the old hymns as she decorated the little red-brick house with greenery, candles, and tiny boxes wrapped in tissue paper of every imaginable hue. It was the first time Elise felt as if she was truly home in this new world.

December brought yet another reason to celebrate— Mama's birthday! It was on the tenth of December, and when Adam told Elise, she immediately planned a fine celebration. But Mama deemed herself "too old and too tired," for the company of people in town, and elected to spend her birthday with her nearest and dearest—namely, her son and his new wife.

"*der Weihnachtsmann* will have to visit you early, Mama," Elise teased.

"Ach, none of that! Father Christmas can keep his visits to you young people. All I ask is for *verheiratete,*" she declared, naming her favorite dumplings, "and as much coffee and *kuchen* as I can hold!"

Elise laughed and agreed. That morning, she rolled up her sleeves, enveloped herself in the largest apron in the house, and began to work on the dumplings as soon as their simple breakfast was cleared away. Mama went to her room to nap, and Adam headed out to work.

"O Tannenbaum," Else hummed, remembering the old song about the Christmas tree. She surveyed the loaded table with pleasure; not only would she make the dumplings in a rich bacon sauce, but there would be a roast and noodles and soups; all the tastiest festive foods she remembered from Germany. It pleased her that, less and less, she thought of Germany as home. Because it wasn't any longer, after all. No, Blue Ridge was now home. The United States. And Adam.

Elise had just tied the roast with string and deftly slipped it into the oven when she heard a rattle and a thump; looking up, she started in surprise to see her husband standing there. For a moment, she was worried, though he'd never objected to German food.

Adam was without hat or coat, and was peering down at the chaos on the kitchen table, his mouth curved into a slight smile. "Busy, I see."

"It's for Mama's birthday," Elise explained, feeling her cheeks color.

"I guessed that." He walked around the table, then popped a few raisins in his mouth. "May I help?"

Elise stared.

He met her eye, then chuckled. "Who do you think has been cooking Mama's birthday lunch all these years, Elise?"

"Well—uh—" Elise was pleased but flustered. In her father's house, no men were ever allowed in the kitchen! "I'm making an apple cake, if you'd like to prepare the fruit?"

Adam nodded, took up a sharp knife, and began to peel.

As they worked, Adam coring, peeling, and slicing apples, sprinkling them with sugar and cinnamon and nutmeg, and lining the enormous pan that his wife indicated, they fell into easy conversation. Adam, for the first time, asked her what Christmases were like in Germany.

"They were simple," Elise admitted. "We didn't do much at home, but all contributed towards our parish celebrations. My father was very enthusiastic about them. We had a huge Tannenbaum celebration every year, with a large Christmas tree and presents for all the children in our community. It was beautiful."

Adam nodded, his eyes thoughtful. "We did much the same in Salzburg. Not so much after we came here. My father, you know, was a forty-eighter."

Elise did not know, but she was quiet, not wanting to interrupt him. He cleared his throat, and continued. "He loved Christmas. When he came to America, he found…new ways to celebrate."

"More American ways?" Elise hoped her words didn't come out sounding harsh. She hadn't intended them that way.

Thankfully, Adam smiled. "Not at first. He was proud to be from Salzburg. But…it was difficult for him. For all of us."

Elise held her breath; Adam seemed on the precipice of opening up to her.

Behavior that seems irrational to us is often a result of hidden hurts.

Adam gave himself a little shake. "Anyway. I have always enjoyed this season. I thank you for taking care of Mama with so much kindness and love."

"You are welcome," she said softly.

"I am honored to have you as a wife," he said, and Elise's eyes dampened a bit at this, and all the more because he said it in German.

"Danke schoen," she whispered.

He smiled. "What would you like for Christmas?"

Elise knew exactly what she wanted; her heart cried for it so loudly she was surprised, in a way, that Adam could not hear it. However, she could not say; instead, she smiled.

"Let's hurry," she said simply. "Mama will want her lunch soon."

"Elise..." he said hesitantly.

She looked up. "Yes, Adam?"

He licked his lips, a troubled look on his handsome face. "My father—" he began, then hesitated, then spoke again, as if forcing himself to do so. "It was... terrible, those first few years. He did not settle where there were many of us, and his failure to adapt led to much..." he stopped, cleared his throat again.

"I've been called...names. Had things thrown. Been treated differently by teachers. This country is one of immigrants, Elise, but—" he paused again. "It is rather unforgiving. I don't want our children to go through—to see—"

Elise's heart was pounding so loudly in her ears, it was hard to hear anything else. "I think I understand," she said quietly, and she did, at long last

He took a deep breath; then he smiled at her. It was as if the moment between them had never happened.

"How would you like," Adam said, "me to attempt a tart, to go with this cake?"

CHAPTER 7

As Christmas grew closer and Adam continued to build support for his impending mayorship in that coming spring, Elise found herself so busy she had little time to think of anything but the particulars of her new life. She had become a fixture of local society, much to her discomfort, but seeing her husband's pleased, proud face more than made up for this. She also increased her work in the Ladies' Aid Society, taking up a collection of children and adults' clothing to be sent to the needy in other settlements, decorating the church for Christmas, and planning the town Christmas party.

One afternoon, when Elise was not present, June volunteered her to organize a Tannenbaum celebration.

"June!" she exclaimed in dismay when she heard of it. "You didn't!"

"I will not allow you to refuse," said her friend. "I had the idea after hearing you speak of your charming Berliner customs at my dinner party, months back. We shall have an absolutely massive tree and songs and presents for the children...it will be lovely, will it not?"

It *would* be lovely, Elise thought wistfully. Lovely and charming and very much like her celebrations in Germany. It warmed her heart to think of it. However, she also thought of Adam and his prickliness and the conversation they had shared at the beginning of the month. "June, I'm not sure—"

"You must be, as everything is arranged!" her friend said merrily. "The tree has been ordered, as have the gifts. All we need is music for Hannah to play, and your husband to make a speech."

A speech! Elise wanted to laugh and cry at the same time. When she returned home, she did both.

"Oh, what a disaster," she said aloud, wiping her cheeks with her apron. She deliberately told Adam nothing. They had been so amiable lately; she hated to spoil that. Besides—

It was Christmas.

Perhaps, she thought, the beauty of the season would melt her husband's cold heart, healing the hurts there.

She certainly hoped it would.

ADAM DISCOVERED HIS WIFE'S SUBTERFUGE AT THE worst possible time, two days before the celebration was planned. Elise was not with him when it happened; she was on the other side of the church, chatting quietly to Hannah Samuels after the day's service. She saw June walk over to her husband to greet him, and Elise thought nothing of it.

It was only after his face contorted with surprise, then darkened, that Elise remembered—and instantly felt ill. The next few minutes were absolutely awful; her husband nodded and smiled and said to June that yes, he was very much looking forward to the Tannenbaum celebration. He even kissed Elise on the cheek when she came over to him; she felt absolutely wretched, knowing it was all a very good act.

When they were outside and finally alone, Adam turned on her in a fury. He did not raise his voice;

nothing in his countenance or carriage was violent. However, his anger was so intense, so oppressive, that it stole Elise's breath from her.

"Adam—"

"Do you think," he said in disbelief, "that I am a fool? That my words, my wishes, are to be disregarded, simply because you think otherwise?"

"Adam, I didn't—"

Elise's heart froze inside of her, for her husband turned his back on her. Coldly. Deliberately.

"You have broken your marital vow to respect and honor me. Go home, Elise," he said.

He did not look back—not when Elise called after him the first time, or the second.

ELISE WANDERED THROUGH TOWN IN A DAZE. THE temperature dropped, and she pulled her coat closer around her but kept walking. The few people still out and about as the sun sank lower in the sky gave her curious looks but said nothing as Elise wandered aimlessly. It was a tiny town. There really was nowhere for her to go besides a few stores, whose owners patiently waited for Elise to browse their wares even though they very likely wanted to close up shop and go home to dinner.

So did she, but she didn't know if she even had a home anymore. What had Adam meant? That coldness in his eyes...it had cut Elise straight to the core. Surely, he had meant the house they shared together. But then again, he'd been so furious that maybe he'd meant for her to pack her bags and somehow find her way back to Germany.

Don't be absurd, a little voice shrilled inside her. *Of course that's not what he meant.*

But, as Elise left the last store and resumed wandering on the increasingly cold streets, his words rang clear as church bells in her ears, but with none of the peace such music usually brought.

You have broken your marital vow to respect and honor me.

Her eyes filled with tears that felt like they froze in her eyes before they could even fall. Elise scrubbed at her bleary vision, stumbling blindly about and not even realizing until a long while after she'd left the town limits and was walking across the vast, snow-dusted prairie. Only it wasn't dusted for long. By the time she came back to some semblance of reality, the snow hung heavy in the air—so much so that when Elise pulled up short, she couldn't see the town limits any longer.

Straining to see through the furious flurries, and shivering violently as the wind blasted over the grasslands and cut through her as harshly as Adam's words, Elise began to realize she was in very big trouble. Germany had terrible snowstorms, of course, but she'd always experienced them within the context of a town. There was always a building to duck into—if not the church, then a school, a store, a blacksmith's shop, or her own home.

Home! her heart cried out, and not for her father's house, as she fought her way forward, not knowing where she was headed but forcing herself to keep moving. She knew if she stopped, it would all be over. And she didn't want it to be. Because in spite of everything, she loved Adam. He was a good man. Surely, he had not cast her out just now...how long ago was it, anyway?

Gradually becoming so numb that her feet felt like the bricks Adam had once used to warm her toes, only far less cozy, Elise prayed. She had absolutely no idea where she was. The song of the river was iced over. She could easily walk straight into it and drown. Or break her neck in an animal burrow. Or freeze to death while just barely still managing to stand upright.

All around her, the landscape was a featureless white and black void. She couldn't even make out trees. It was like she was walking in some kind of twisted painting, perhaps leaving footprints behind that zigzagged erratically, though Elise couldn't have seen them even if she bothered to try to look.

Please, God. She took another step. *Help me.* Yet another step. She folded her arms tight against the cold.

I don't want to die.

As she staggered forward, losing her scarf to a gust of wind so her face was mercilessly exposed to the storm, faces flashed through her mind—her father's face, her aunt's face, kind Mrs. Brown's face, June's face, and finally—Adam. Dear, hurt, angry Adam, who Elise did not fully understand, but who she loved.

I do love him. And that was why it all hurt so much. The thought that their last words had been spoken in anger scared her far more than death. God would take her to heaven—of that Elise was sure, though she had no intention of giving up. But Adam would have to live with his angry words, and she knew he'd feel guilty. He was a good, dear man in spite of his scars, and if she died like this, it would only add to the burden of grief and anger and misplaced guilt he already felt.

I'll never be able to tell him my Christmas surprise, Elise thought sadly, wrapping her arms more tightly around her midriff and walking on and on and on and on. *God, please help me. Have mercy.*

Finally, it became too much. She didn't quite realize when she sank to her knees in a heavy pile of snow. Didn't remember lying down in the cold dampness that soon, strangely, became deliciously warm. Didn't feel the water saturating her every inch as Elise gave herself over to the darkness.

Just a few minutes...then I'll keep on moving...

"Elise!"

In the darkness of her dream, Elise smiled. Here at the end, Adam had come to be with her. It was good. There were worse ways to leave the world behind.

"Elise!"

Rough, frantic hands grabbed at her. Loud voices filled her ears, even louder than the roar of the storm.

Frowning, Elise clung to her cloak of silence and warmth. *No. Let me be. It's peaceful in this place. Go away.*

"Elise, I won't let you die on me. I love you. I'm sorry. Elise, *fight*, please!"

As she drifted away again, she knew for certain she was dreaming because every single word Dream Adam spoke was in German.

CHAPTER 8

Waking was far more difficult than going to sleep, it turned out. As Elise gradually began to revive, it was with a cry of pain as shards of glass seemed to cut into every part of her body.

"Hush," a deep, gruff voice murmured nearby. "That's just the circulation returning. It will hurt for a while, yes, but it means you'll be fine, the doctor said. You'll be fine. Fine. Open your eyes, my love. Please."

But he was still speaking German, so Elise knew she was still in some form of dream. As she began to allow herself to slip away once more, big hands grasped her shoulders, and she felt warm breath on her face. "Open your eyes, Elise. Don't give up. Please. I was wrong. I'm so terribly, terribly sorry. Please, come back to me."

The grief in the German words was so potent that she managed to find the strength to just inch her eyes open, however painful every move was. And there, as the room swam into view—the living room, from what Elise could vaguely make out, complete with a blazing fire a few feet away—she found Adam gazing down at her, tears in his eyes.

As he saw her start to revive, his face contorted, and he cupped her cheeks in his hands, still speaking her native language. "My love. My life. I'm so sorry. I never meant to drive you away, much less out into a storm. Please forgive me. Please be well again. I love you, Elise. I need you."

"You'll overwhelm her," another German voice said from nearby, this one female.

Painfully, still lost in confusion, Elise managed to turn her aching head just enough to spot Mama sitting in a rocking chair, swathed in blankets. The old woman gave her a tender smile. "Take your time, dear. When you're ready, there's spiced tea to help warm you back to life once more. You gave us all quite a scare."

"What...happened..." Elise managed to croak out as Adam carefully eased her upright on the couch so she could take a few sips of Mama's tea.

"We fought," Adam explained, his face coming more clearly into view as Elise's sight cleared gradually. "I said things. Things I didn't mean and things that you misunderstood. I've been wrong, Elise. You should not have to pretend not to have roots in another country. That is where you began as a person. The person I love."

His tender words warmed her far more deeply than any tea ever could.

"We can find a way to be American-German," Adam went on, pressing her hands tightly and kissing each one in turn. "It's not a betrayal of either country. And if people make fun, so be it."

Elise blinked back suddenly scalding tears. "How did...you find me?"

"God," Mama said simply, and Adam added,

"When you didn't come home, it took me a while to realize what must have happened. Then I had the whole town immediately up in arms, searching for you." He switched to English, which helped Elise feel a little more oriented to time and place. "Your footprints were lost in the snow, Elise. The only reason I found you was because Jeb Winters spotted your bright red scarf. It was almost buried, but not entirely. I knew it couldn't be too far from you, and it wasn't."

His voice broke slightly, and he guided her to take another sip of tea. "You were outside for at least an hour. Doc says any longer, and you'd either have died or lost some of your limbs."

Elise winced at the thought, and also at the pain as her hands and feet gradually came back to life. "Adam," she whispered, "I'm sorry too. The celebration—I honestly didn't mean to be disrespectful. June—"

"Hush," Adam cut her off, leaning in and startling Elise with a tender kiss even though Mama was nearby. "I was in the wrong. You were not. Now rest, my love. Just rest. We have a celebration to attend tomorrow, and even if I have to carry you, you'll be there, I promise."

She faded back to sleep, a smile on her face.

❧

THE NEXT DAY, STILL IN PAIN AND DEEPLY fatigued, but grateful to God and delighted to be still here to be able to take part in celebrations, Elise sat in the front seat of the schoolhouse assembly room, wrapped tightly in furs. The Christmas tree she'd helped the ladies decorate loomed lofty and full, filling the room with its fresh piney scent, and brightly wrapped packages hung from every branch.

With the church service over, they'd all gathered there to sing and eat, though Elise had no appetite just yet, and her voice was too raspy to even consider raising in song. Her friends solicitously waited on her hand and foot as they all rejoiced in God's grace. At one point, Elise felt Adam shift from her side, where he'd sat all morning. Confused, she followed him with her gaze as he walked to the front of the room and cleared his throat.

"Will you all join me in prayer, please?" Then he bowed his head, as did they all. *Our father who art in heaven. Vater unser im Himmel, geheiligt werde dein Name...*"

Elise wept quietly with joy, unnoticed by the others as they all recited the familiar words in English. Not one person complained or interrupted as Adam finished praying. When he finished, though, he didn't sit back down. Instead, he cleared his throat once more and began to speak. He spoke of the *Christkind*, and writing letters to him as a child. He spoke of the importance of the tree in their culture, and of Christmases past in the old country. He spoke of his mother, and the legacy she had left him.

Finally he spoke of Elise, and the love she had brought to his household, and the hopes he had for their marriage.

Elise sat with eyes that were too full to see and a throat that was too hoarse to speak, and knew that she was finally, finally, well and truly home for good.

There were sweets after Adam finished speaking, rejoining Elise and giving her a soft, sweet kiss, and there was coffee and laughter and children opening their gifts in delight, strewing colored tissue paper all over the floor. Mama watched it all beneath her new cap of Brussels lace, smiling more broadly than Elise had ever seen.

It was all so perfect and so lovely but, still weak from her close call yesterday, Elise felt herself start to nod off, and Adam swept her up then and carried her home, tucking her into their big warm bed with several hot water bottles and thick, heavy blankets.

And Elise did, but not before she managed to just whisper her Christmas present to him. "Adam...next year we'll have a little one to help us celebrate this most precious of seasons."

That was all she managed before becoming completely lost in sleep once more. Adam was left staring at his beautiful wife, thinking hard of love, Christmas miracles, and of a future that suddenly seemed brighter than it ever had before.

To continue enjoying Mail Order Bride Christmas Miracles Romance Complete Series. **(4 Book Series)**

Katie Wyatt with Ada Oakley Mail Order Bride Christmas Miracles Romance series

ROYCE CARDIFF PUBLISHING HOUSE PRESENTS other wonderful clean, wholesome and inspiring romance short stories titles for your entertainment. Many are value boxset and as always FREE to Kindle Unlimited readers.

COMPLETE SERIES
Sweet Western Romance

KATIE WYATT, BRENDA CLEMMONS AND ELLEN ANDERSON

katie wyatt box set complete series

Sweet Frontier Cowboys Complete Series Collection (A Novel Christian Romance Series)

Katie Wyatt Mega Box Set Series (12 Mega Box Set Series)

THANK YOU SO MUCH FOR READING MY BOOK. I sincerely hope you enjoyed every bit reading it. I had fun creating it and will surely create more.

Your positive reviews are very helpful to other reader, it only takes a few moments. They can be left at Amazon.

www.amazon.com/Katie-Wyatt/e/B011IN7AF0

WANT FREE BOOKS EVERY WEEK? WHO DOESN'T!

. . .

Become a preferred reader and we'll not only send you free reads, but you'll also receive updates about new releases.

So you'll be among the first to dive into our latest new books, full of adventure, heartwarming romances, and characters so real they jump off the page.

It's absolutely free and you don't need to do anything at all to qualify except go to.

PREFERRED READ FREE READS

http:/katieWyattBooks.com/readersgroup

KATIE WYATT IS 25% AMERICAN SIOUX INDIAN. Born and raised in Arizona, she has traveled and camped extensively through California, Arizona, Nevada, Mexico, and New Mexico. Looking at the incredible night sky and the giant Saguaro cacti, she has dreamed of what it would be like to live in the early pioneer times.

Spending time with a relative of the great Wyatt Earp, also named Wyatt Earp, Katie was mesmerized and inspired by the stories he told of bygone times. This historical interest in the old West became the inspiration for her Western romance novels.

Her books are a mixture of actual historical facts and events mixed with action and humor, challenges and adventures. The characters in Katie's clean romance novels draw from her own experiences and are so real that they almost jump off the pages. You feel like you're walking beside them through all the ups and downs of their lives. As the stories unfold, you'll find yourself both laughing and crying. The endings will never fail to leave you feeling warm inside.

ADA OAKLEY IS AN AMERICAN-born ITALIAN, who has lived most of her life in Dallas Texas and has traveled to many countries. She has been an avid reader and a lover of western movies since her teenage years, so she decided to pursue a writing career.

Ada loves writing Western Romance and Mail Order Bride stories about the courageous women who traveled alone to the Wild West with nothing but hope and strong faith in God.

Her inspirations are her dogs and three lovely cats! So if you're up to reading an excellent feel good clean romance story, her stories are highly recommended.